# THE SEEING STICK

By Jane Yolen   Pictures by Remy Charlip and Demetra Maraslis

THOMAS Y. CROWELL COMPANY  NEW YORK

For Ann Beneduce
with ten years of thanks and love—
Jane
And to the pleasure of new beginnings—
Demetra and Remy

OTHER BOOKS BY JANE YOLEN

The Bird of Time
The Girl Who Loved the Wind
The Wizard Islands
The Boy Who Had Wings
The Girl Who Cried Flowers and Other Tales
Rainbow Rider
The Magic Three of Solatia
The Transfigured Hart
The Moon Ribbon and Other Tales
Milkweed Days

COPYRIGHT© 1977 BY JANE YOLEN
ILLUSTRATIONS COPYRIGHT© 1977 BY
REMY CHARLIP AND DEMETRA MARASLIS
ALL RIGHTS RESERVED. EXCEPT FOR USE IN A REVIEW, THE REPRO-
DUCTION OR UTILIZATION OF THIS WORK IN ANY FORM OR BY ANY
ELECTRONIC, MECHANICAL, OR OTHER MEANS, NOW KNOWN OR
HEREAFTER INVENTED, INCLUDING XEROGRAPHY, PHOTOCOPYING,
AND RECORDING, AND IN ANY INFORMATION STORAGE AND
RETRIEVAL SYSTEM IS FORBIDDEN WITHOUT THE WRITTEN PER-
MISSION OF THE PUBLISHER. PUBLISHED SIMULTANEOUSLY IN
CANADA BY FITZHENRY & WHITESIDE LIMITED, TORONTO.
MANUFACTURED IN THE UNITED STATES OF AMERICA.
LIBRARY OF CONGRESS CATALOGING IN PUBLICATION DATA
YOLEN, JANE H   THE SEEING STICK.
SUMMARY: RELATES HOW AN OLD MAN TEACHES THE EMPEROR'S
BLIND DAUGHTER TO SEE.   [1. BLIND—FICTION.
2. CHINA—FICTION] I. CHARLIP, REMY, AND
DEMETRA MARASLIS.   II. TITLE.   PZ7.Y78Sc   [E]   75-6946
ISBN 0-690-00455-9   0-690-00596-2 (CQR)

Once in the ancient walled citadel of Peking
there lived an emperor who had only one daughter,
and her name was Hwei Ming.
Now this daughter had carved ivory combs
to smoothe back her long black hair.
Her tiny feet were encased in embroidered slippers,
and her robes were woven of the finest silks.
But rather than making her happy,
such possessions made her sad.
For Hwei Ming was blind,
and all the beautiful handcrafts in the kingdom
brought her no pleasure at all.
Her father was also sad
that his only daughter was blind,
but he could not cry for her.
He was the emperor after all,
and had given up weeping over such things
when he ascended the throne.
Yet still he had hope
that one day Hwei Ming might be able to see.
So he resolved that if someone could help her,
such a person would be rewarded
with a fortune in jewels.

He sent word of his offer
to the inner and outer cities of Peking
and to all the towns and villages
for hundreds of miles around.
Monks came, of course,
with their prayers and prayer wheels,
for they thought in this way
to help Hwei Ming see.
Magician-priests came, of course,
with their incantations and spells,
for they thought in this way
to help Hwei Ming see.
Physicians came, of course,
with their potions and pins,
for they thought in this way
to help Hwei Ming see.
But nothing could help.
Hwei Ming had been blind from the day of her birth,
and no one could effect a cure.

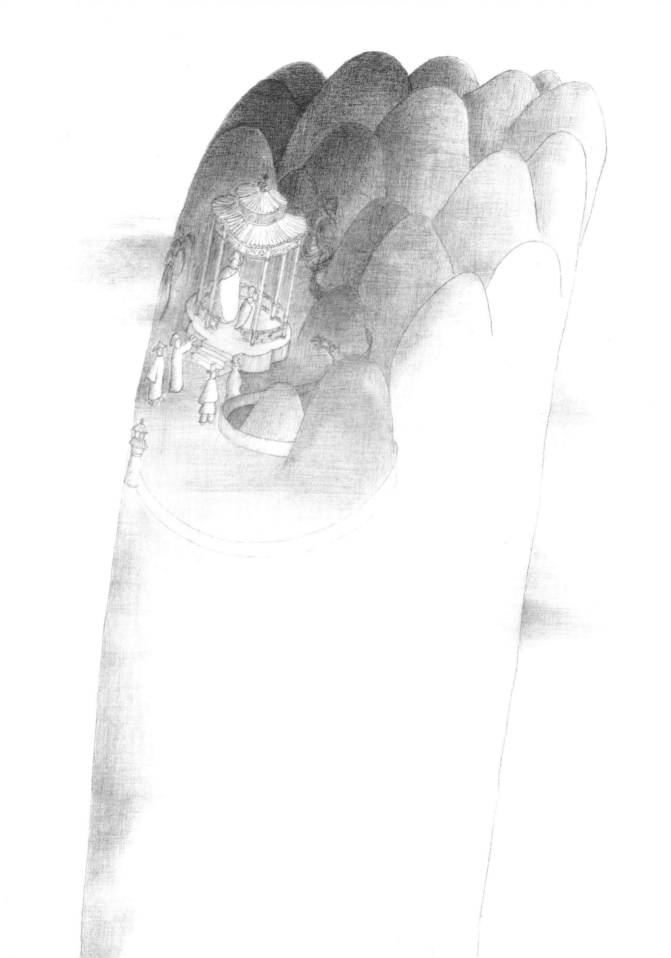

Now one day
an old man, who lived far away
in the south country,
heard tales of the blind princess.
He heard of the emperor's offer.
And so he took his few possessions—
a long walking stick,
made from a single piece of golden wood,
and his whittling knife—
and started up the road.
The sun rose hot on his right side
and the sun set cool on his left
as he made his way north to Peking
to help the princess see.

At last the old man,
his clothes tattered by his travels,
stopped by the gate of the Outer City.
The guards at the gate
did not want to let such a ragged old man in.
"Grandfather, go home.
There is nothing here for such as you," they said.
The old man touched their faces in turn
with his rough fingers.
"So young," he said,
"and already so old."
He turned as if to go.
Then he propped his walking stick
against his side
and reached into his shirt
for his whittling knife.
"What are you doing, grandfather?"
called out one of the guards
when he saw the old man bring out the knife.
"I am going to show you my stick, "
said the old man.
"For it is a stick that sees."
"Grandfather, that is nonsense,"
said the second guard.
"That stick can see no farther
than can the emperor's daughter."

"Just so, just so,"
said the old man.
"But stranger things have happened."
And so saying,
he picked up the stick
and stropped the knife blade back and forth
three times to sharpen its edge.
As the guards watched
from the gate in the wall,
the old man told them
how he had walked the many miles
through villages and towns
till he came with his seeing stick
to the walls of Peking.
And as he told them his tale,
he pointed to the pictures in the stick:
an old man,
his home,
the long walk,
the walls of Peking.
And as they watched further,
he began to cut their portraits into the wood.
The two guards looked at each other
in amazement and delight.
They were flattered at their likenesses
on the old man's stick.
Indeed, they had never witnessed such carving skill.

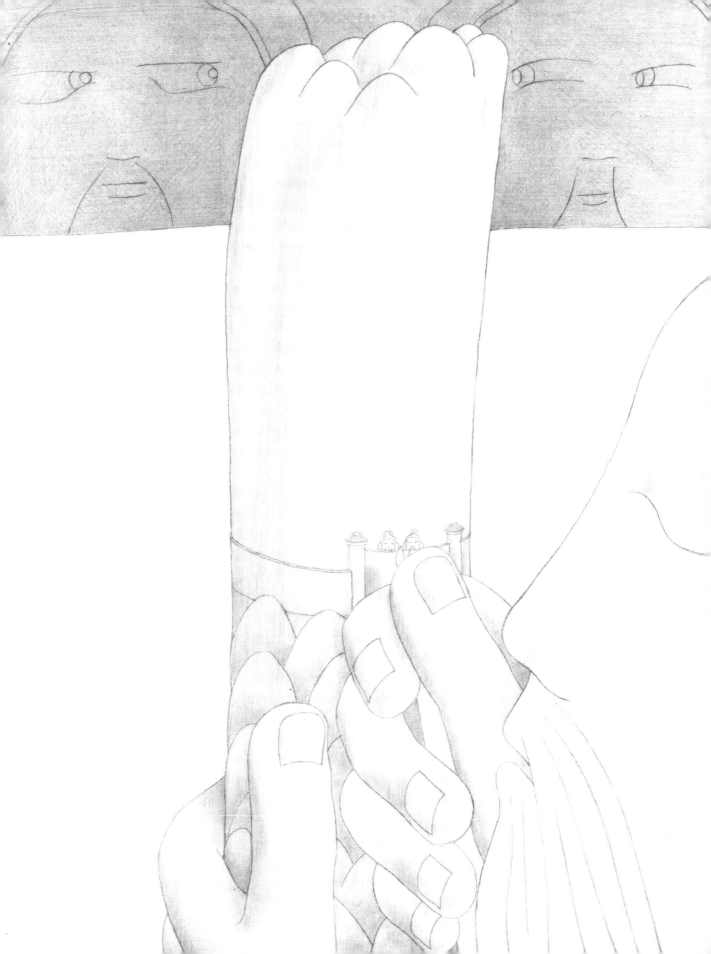

"Surely this is something
the guards at the wall
of the Inner City should see," they said.
So, taking the old man by the arm,
they guided him
through the streets of the Outer City,
past flower peddlers and rice sellers,
past silk weavers and jewel merchants,
up to the great stone walls.
When the guards of the Inner City
saw the seeing stick,
they were surprised and delighted.
"Carve our faces, too,"
they begged like children.
And laughing,
and touching their faces
as any fond grandfather would,
the old man did as they bid.
In no time at all,
the guards of the Inner City took the old man by his arm
and led him to the wall of the Innermost City
and in through the gate
to the great wooden doors of the Imperial Palace.

Now when the guards arrived
in the throne room of the Imperial Palace
leading the old man by the arm,
it happened that the emperor's blind daughter,
Hwei Ming,
was sitting by his side,
her hands clasped before her,
silent, sightless, and still.
As the guards finished telling
of the wonderful pictures carved on the golden stick,
the princess clapped her hands.
"Oh, I wish I could see that wondrous stick," she said.
"Just so, just so," said the old man.
"And I will show it to you.
For it is no ordinary piece of wood,
but a stick that sees."
"What nonsense," said her father
in a voice so low it was almost a growl.
But the princess did not hear him.
She had already bent toward
the sound of the old man's voice.
"A seeing stick?"

The old man did not say anything for a moment.
Then he leaned forward
and petted Hwei Ming's head
and caressed her cheek.
For though she was a princess,
she was still a child.
Then the old man began to tell again
the story of his long journey to Peking.
He introduced each character and object—
the old man,
the guards,
the great walls,
the Innermost City.
And then he carved the wooden doors,
the Imperial Palace,
the princess, into the golden wood.
When he finished,
the old man reached out
for the princess' small hands.
He took her tiny fingers in his
and placed them on the stick.
Finger on finger,
he helped her trace the likenesses.
"Feel the long flowing hair of the princess,"
the old man said.
"Grown as she herself has grown,
straight and true."
And Hwei Ming touched the carved stick.
"Now feel your own long hair," he said.
And she did.

"Feel the lines in the old man's face," he said.
"From years of worry and years of joy."
He thrust the stick into her hands again.
And the princess' slim fingers
felt the carved stick.
Then he put her fingers onto his face
and traced the same lines there.
It was the first time
the princess had touched another person's face
since she was a very small girl.
The princess jumped up from her throne
and thrust her hands before her.
"Guards, O guards," she cried out.
"Come here to me."
And the guards lifted up their faces
to the Princess Hwei Ming's hands.
Her fingers,
like little breezes,
brushed their eyes and noses and mouths,
and then found each one on the carved stick.

Hwei Ming turned to her father,
the emperor,
who sat straight and tall
and unmoving on his great throne.
She reached out
and her fingers ran eagerly
through his hair
and down his nose and cheek
and rested curiously on a tear they found there.
And that was strange, indeed,
for had not the emperor
given up crying over such things
when he ascended the throne?

They brought her
through the streets of the city, then,
the emperor in the lead.
And Princess Hwei Ming
touched men and women
and children as they passed.
Till at last
she stood before the great walls of Peking
and felt the stones themselves.
Then she turned to the old man.
Her voice was bright
and full of laughter.
"Tell me another tale," she said.
"Tomorrow, if you wish," he replied.

For each tomorrow
as long as he lived,
the old man dwelt
in the Innermost City,
where only the royal family stays.
The emperor rewarded him
with a fortune in jewels,
but the old man gave them all away.
Every day
he told the princess a story.
Some were tales as ancient
as the city itself.
Some were as new
as the events of the day.
And each time
he carved wonderful images
in the stick of golden wood.
As the princess listened,
she grew eyes
on the tips of her fingers.
At least that is what
she told the other blind children
whom she taught to see as she saw.
Certainly it was as true
as saying she had a seeing stick.
But the blind Princess Hwei Ming
believed that both things were true.
And so did all the blind children
in her city of Peking.

And so did the blind old man.